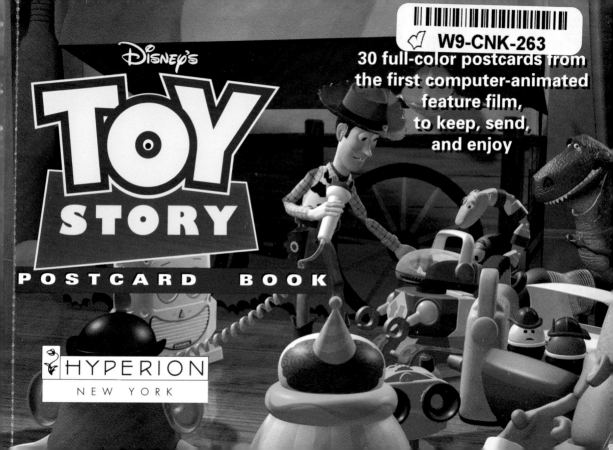

DISNEP'S

TOY STORY

POSTCARD BOOK

30 full-color postcards from
the first computer-animated
feature film,
to keep, send,
and enjoy

HYPERION
NEW YORK

For information address Hyperion, 114 Fifth Avenue, New York, New York 10011.

ISBN 0-7868-8138-0
First Edition
10 9 8 7 6 5 4 3 2 1

DESIGN & PRODUCTION BY ROBERT BULL DESIGN

INTRODUCTION

Set in a world where a toy's greatest fear is being replaced by newer toys, *Toy Story* is a comedy adventure that takes viewers of all ages on a journey with two rival toys. Woody is a pull-string talking cowboy and Buzz Lightyear is a superhero space action figure. The mismatched duo must learn to set

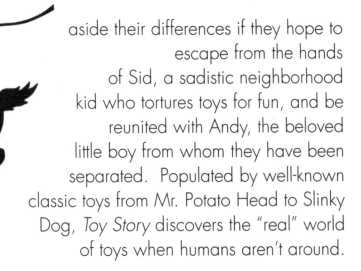

aside their differences if they hope to escape from the hands of Sid, a sadistic neighborhood kid who tortures toys for fun, and be reunited with Andy, the beloved little boy from whom they have been separated. Populated by well-known classic toys from Mr. Potato Head to Slinky Dog, *Toy Story* discovers the "real" world of toys when humans aren't around.

"Hey, Etch! Draw!"
Woody challenges
Etch-A-Sketch.

A HYPERION POSTCARD BOOK

Slinky Dog prepares for a game of checkers with Woody.

★
★
★
★
★
★
★
★
★
★
★
★
★
★
★
★
★
★
★
★

A HYPERION POSTCARD BOOK

"Whaddya say I get
someone else to watch
the sheep tonight?"
says Bo Peep, flirting.

A HYPERION POSTCARD BOOK

Rex and Slinky Dog
go to the staff
meeting.

A HYPERION POSTCARD BOOK

Woody announces
Andy's birthday party
at the staff meeting.

★
★
★
★
★
★
★
★
★
★
★
★
★
★
★
★
★
★
★
★
★
★
★

A HYPERION POSTCARD BOOK

Mr. Potato Head
is more than
ambidextrous.

A HYPERION POSTCARD BOOK

The toys agree to
stay calm if Woody
sends out the troops.

A HYPERION POSTCARD BOOK

The army men freeze
in position as Andy's
mom comes by.

A HYPERION POSTCARD BOOK

Mr. Potato Head
loses face in front
of all the other toys.

A HYPERION POSTCARD BOOK

Camouflaged in
a potted plant, the
sergeant monitors
the birthday party.

A HYPERION POSTCARD BOOK

Woody crawls out from under Andy's bed after being knocked to the floor.

A HYPERION POSTCARD BOOK

Woody climbs back onto the bed to check out Andy's new toy.

A HYPERION POSTCARD BOOK

"I am Buzz Lightyear.
I come in peace."

A HYPERION POSTCARD BOOK

Buzz tries to use his
wrist communicator:
"Star Command—
come in. Do you read me?"

A HYPERION POSTCARD BOOK

Rex asks,
"Mr. Lightyear, what
does a space ranger
actually do?"

A HYPERION POSTCARD BOOK

"He's not a space ranger," insists Woody.

A HYPERION POSTCARD BOOK

Disney's
TOY STORY

Mr. Potato Head eyes
Hamm during a serious
game of cards.

A HYPERION POSTCARD BOOK

"Listen Lightsnack...
stop with this spaceman
thing, it's getting
on my nerves."

A HYPERION POSTCARD BOOK

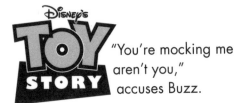

"You're mocking me aren't you," accuses Buzz.

A HYPERION POSTCARD BOOK

The toys at the window
look down into Sid's
backyard.

A HYPERION POSTCARD BOOK

Hamm and Potato Head look accusingly at Woody.

A HYPERION POSTCARD BOOK

Rex tells Bo that
there aren't enough
monkeys in the bar-
rel to rescue Buzz.

A HYPERION POSTCARD BOOK

Woody gets the scare
of his life when he
discovers Babyface.

A HYPERION POSTCARD BOOK

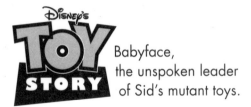

Babyface,
the unspoken leader
of Sid's mutant toys.

A HYPERION POSTCARD BOOK

Woody hides behind
Buzz as he shoots his
laser at the Mutant
Toys

A HYPERION POSTCARD BOOK

The Mutant Toys try to
right Sid's wrongs.

A HYPERION POSTCARD BOOK